Library of Congress Cataloging in Publication Data

Yamanushi, Toshiko,
    The nutcracker.
        SUMMARY: A little girl travels with the Nutcracker
Prince to the Land of Cake and Candy.
        Translation of Kurumi-wari ningyo.
    [1. Fairy tales]   I. Hoffmann, Ernst Theodor
Amadeus, 1776-1822.   Nussknacker und Mausekönig.
II. Horiuchi, Seiichi, 1932-   illus. III. Title.
PZ8.Y25Nu3   895.6'3'5 [E]   74-6479
ISBN 0-8193-0743-2
ISBN 0-8193-0744-0 (lib. bdg.)

The Nutcracker

Retold by Toshiko Yamanushi   *Illustrated by Seiichi Horiuchi*

English version by Alvin Tresselt

Parents' Magazine Press / New York

Such excitement!

It was Christmas Eve.

The house was filled with aunts and uncles,
cousins and friends.

The good sounds and smells of Christmas
were everywhere.

In the place of honor stood a beautiful Christmas tree.

And when it was time to open the presents, Maria
got a lovely doll with eyes that opened and closed.

A brand new party dress, too.

Fritz was given a proud white horse
and a fine set of toy soldiers.

Then, way under the tree, Maria found
an odd-looking little wooden man.
"What a funny, angry face he has," she cried.
"He will be my favorite toy."
"His mouth must be for cracking nuts," said Fritz.
"Watch. When I move this lever it opens and closes."
They took turns cracking walnuts and hazelnuts
and tasty sweet pecans.
Then Fritz tried a nut that was much too big.
Crrrack! went the poor little man's jaw.
"Look what you've done!" Maria cried.
"Now my best present is broken!"
"Don't worry," said her mother,
"we'll fix him in the morning.
It's long past your bedtime."

Maria tenderly put the nutcracker
into her doll's bed in the toy cabinet.
Fritz lined up his new soldiers on the shelves above
and went off to his room.
Though it was very late, Maria stayed
to comfort her nutcracker.

The clock struck twelve.

Suddenly, Maria heard squeaks from all directions.

Holding up her lamp, she saw giant mice
racing across the room!

In the lead was a Mouse King, carrying a long sharp sword.

He had seven heads.

"Help! Help!" cried Maria, falling back against
the toy shelves.

At that instant, all the toys came to life.
The horses reared, the soldiers lined up,
the drummers drummed, and the cannons
rolled into position.

The Nutcracker, too, leapt into action.

"Come on, men," he commanded. "Get the mice!"

Down they sprang to the floor, ready for battle.

With the sound of drums in their ears,
they charged. Again and again the cannons roared,
but their cannonballs were only made of sugar.

The soldiers proved powerless against the mice.
"Capture the general!" ordered the Mouse King.
His followers surrounded the Nutcracker, who
could do nothing to save himself.

All the while
Maria had been watching the fierce battle.
When she saw her beloved Nutcracker in danger,
she took off her slipper
and threw it as hard as she could,
right at the Mouse King.
In a flash, the mice all disappeared.
What had happened?
Maria fainted.

From far off
she seemed to hear someone calling her name.
Slowly she opened her eyes,
and there stood the Nutcracker beside her.
"Ah," he said, "I'm so glad you are all right.
As a reward for saving my life,
I will take you to a magical kingdom."
With that, the doors of the wardrobe flew open
and a golden staircase appeared.

Together they climbed it
until they reached a great meadow,
dazzling with bright-colored flowers.
At the far side stood a wide gate,
on top of which a band of monkeys
played a lively tune of welcome.
As they passed through,
Maria discovered it was all made of cake.

Beyond was a forest,
its trees laden with candies
and bonbons of every size and shape.
Soon they came to a small clearing where
a group of shepherds and shepherdesses

sat Maria in a golden chair. They played
flutes and danced in her honor.
When their performance was done, the Nutcracker said,
"Now we must hurry!" and he led the way to a broad lake.
The air filled with the scent of a million roses.

"This is Rose Lake," explained Maria's guide.
Waiting at the shore was a golden seashell chariot
drawn by two frisky dolphins.
As they glided across the water,
a chorus of little people sang sweet songs to them.

In the distance loomed the towers of a great city,
with buildings made of every kind of cake
and trimmed with candies, nuts and sweetmeats.
It was the capital of the Land of Cake and Candy.
As Maria and the Nutcracker entered,
they were greeted by guards in silver uniforms.

"Welcome home, dear Prince," said the mayor. For
the Nutcracker was none other than the Prince
of the Land of Cake and Candy! Everyone cheered
as he and Maria rode through the streets to the
great Candy Castle.

Once inside, they were met by a retinue of servants.
Four beautiful princesses rushed to embrace their brother.
The Nutcracker explained how Maria had bravely rescued
him from the Mouse King. Each princess in turn gave
the little girl a kiss and thanked her for her good deed.

Then they all went into the banquet hall,
where a great feast was held in their honor.
But suddenly, Maria felt strange.
The room turned round and round
and slowly disappeared.

The next thing she knew, Maria was in her very own bed.

Her mother and father were bending over her.

"We have just carried you in," whispered her mother.

"We found you on the floor by the toy shelf,

hugging your nutcracker. And he isn't broken at all!"

Maria smiled. "I know," she said.

Then she told of her adventures in the Land of Cake

and Candy.

"What a strange and lovely dream you had,"

said her father. "But go back to sleep now.

It will soon be Christmas morning."